A HOLE IN
HER POCKET
AND OTHER STORIES

A Hole In Her Pocket

and Other Stories

by
ENID BLYTON

Illustrated by
Sally Gregory

AWARD PUBLICATIONS

For further information on Enid Blyton please visit *www.blyton.com*

ISBN 978-1-84135-449-1

Illustrations copyright © Award Publications Limited

First published 1951 as *A Picnic Party with Enid Blyton*
by Hodder and Stoughton Limited

First published by Award Publications Limited 1987
This edition first published 2005

Published by Award Publications Limited,
The Old Riding School, The Welbeck Estate,
Worksop, Nottinghamshire, S80 3LR

13 6

Printed in the United Kingdom

CONTENTS

1

What a Funny Thing to Do

Janet was pleased because Auntie Laura had given her some Shirley poppy seeds to plant in her garden.

'Wait for a fine day, just after rain,' said Auntie Laura. 'Then shake them gently out of the envelope into a sunny patch of ground, cover them up with fine soil, and wait for them to grow.'

Janet shook them in the packet. They made a nice dry, rustly noise.

'They are seeds I took from my own Shirley poppies for you last summer,' said Auntie Laura. 'They were such fine ones, and made so much seed. I have some for myself, some for you and some for your cousin John. He is going to plant his, too. I have given him some in an envelope, just like yours. You will

7

have to see whose come up first.'

Janet hoped hers would. John lived next door, so she would easily be able to see if hers came up first.

'Don't plant them just yet,' said Auntie Laura. 'It's a bit too early. And do keep your seeds carefully, Janet – don't lose them. You can be such a careless little girl, you know.'

Janet knew. People were always telling her how careless she was. She lost things. She broke things. She made silly mistakes. But she really *would* be careful with her poppy seeds. She went to put them in the drawer of her dressing-table, where her handkerchiefs, stockings and brooches were. They would be quite safe there.

The next day Janet went to a party, and every child had a dip in a bran-tub. It was very exciting. You put your hand down into the bran and felt about. Soon your fingers touched a parcel, and you could feel it and see if you thought it was anything exciting. If you didn't think so you could feel about again and find something else.

Janet felt about and found a thin little parcel that felt quite exciting. So she pulled it out of the tub and undid the paper.

'Oh! It's a necklace!' she said in delight. 'Isn't it pretty? It's made of tiny beads of all colours! I *shall* love wearing it.'

She put it on, and it looked very pretty on her silk party frock. Janet felt very grand.

But, as usual, she was careless, and as she danced round playing musical chairs she caught her hand in the new little necklace and snapped it.

In a second the little coloured beads ran all over the place. Some went down Janet's neck, some fell on the carpet, some dropped on to a chair.

'Oh, my lovely necklace that I got out of the bran-tub,' said Janet, almost in tears.

'Don't cry,' said a grown-up. 'We'll soon find the beads for you, then you can thread them together again when you get home. That will be a nice thing to do. Look, here are some, and there are some more.'

All the children helped to find the little glass beads. 'What shall we do with them?' they said, holding them in their hands. 'Where shall we put them?'

'I'll find an envelope,' said the grown-up, and went to a desk. She came back with a white envelope, and everyone put the beads into it. It was licked up and stuck. Janet took it and put it into her pocket.

'Thank you,' she said. 'I'll thread them when I have time at home, and make a lovely necklace again.'

When she got home she told her mother all about the broken necklace, and wanted to thread it before she went to bed. But Mother wouldn't let her.

'Oh, no,' she said, 'it's very late, dear. You can thread the beads tomorrow. Put them into your drawer and you will keep them safe there.'

12

So Janet went up to bed and popped the envelope of beads into her dressing-table drawer. Now there were two envelopes there – one with poppy seeds in and one with glass beads.

Janet forgot about the beads, and there they stayed, hidden in their envelope. Then there came a fine sunny day after a day of showers, and the gardener began to plant his seeds in the garden.

'Haven't you any seeds to plant, Missie?' he said to Janet. 'You ought to plant them today if you have. It's just right.'

'Oh, yes; I've got some Shirley poppy seeds that my Auntie Laura gave me,' said Janet remembering. 'I'll go and get them.'

As she was running indoors her cousin John popped his head over the wall. 'Janet, Janet!' he called. 'I am planting my seeds today that Auntie Laura gave me. Are you planting yours?'

'Yes,' said Janet. 'Oh, good, we'll

13

plant them the same day, so they ought to come up the same day. We'll watch and see.'

She ran upstairs in a hurry and opened her dressing-table drawer. She took out the first envelope she saw – but it wasn't the one with the seeds in. It was the one with the beads in.

Janet rushed downstairs and into the garden. She went to her own little patch. It had one rose tree in, one lupin plant just coming up, one plant of primroses all out, and at one side was a little bare patch where Janet meant to plant her poppy seeds.

14

She raked it over a little to make it fine, for she knew that seeds must be planted in a very fine soil. Then she scraped back some of the earth and made a place ready to shake the seeds on to.

She slit open the envelope, bent over the patch of moist warm earth and began to shake the contents of the envelope on to the ground. She was rather surprised to see that the seeds were all colours. 'Oh,' she said, 'I suppose they're all colours because Shirley poppies are all colours, too. What dear little seeds! I do like them. I hope they grow well.'

15

Janet planted all the beads out of the envelope, and she really thought they were seeds. She covered them up with fine soil, and then called to John over the wall. 'I've planted my poppy seeds. They were so pretty, all colours of the rainbow,'

John was surprised. 'Mine weren't,' he said. 'Mine were all little black things.'

Two or three weeks went by and the children watched eagerly for their seeds to come up. Janet went to see every day if any little green spike had pushed up. But none had.

Then one day John gave a squeal of delight. 'Janet! Janet! All my poppy seeds are up! They are as green as anything. Are yours?'

Janet looked, and she was very disappointed to find none of hers showing at all. 'I expect mine will be up tomorrow,' she said.

But they weren't. They weren't showing the next day either,or the next. Janet couldn't bear to keep hearing

John shout out how well his were growing, so tall and sturdy and green. Why didn't hers grow? She had planted them the same day as John's!

She told Auntie Laura, and Auntie was puzzled. 'It's funny,' she said. 'They were just the same seeds.'

17

Janet looked as if she was going to cry. 'Now, don't be a baby,' said her mother. 'Find something to do whilst Auntie and I have a talk. What about that necklace of beads you broke at Hilda's party? You have never threaded them have you? Wouldn't it be a good idea to thread them now, then you can show Auntie how pretty they are.'

'Oh, yes,' said Janet, cheering up. 'I quite forgot all about the beads. They are in my dressing-table drawer. I'll get them.'

She ran up to her room, scrabbled about in her drawer for the envelope, found it and ran downstairs again. She slit open the envelope to show her aunt the beads. But how strange – there were no beads inside – only funny little black things, like seeds!

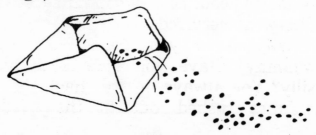

'Where have the beads gone?' said Janet, in surprise. 'Oh, Mummy, look what my beads have turned into! They've gone ugly and horrid – they're not beads any more. I can't thread them.'

Mummy and Auntie Laura looked. Then Auntie laughed. 'Silly child! These are seeds – they look like poppy seeds, too. Are you sure you planted your poppy seeds? These look exactly like the ones I gave you – and this looks like the envelope, too.'

Janet stared at it. Oh dear – oh dear – could she possibly have been silly enough to plant beads instead of seeds? No, she really couldn't!

Then she remembered what bright colours the seeds that she had planted had been – yes, they must have been beads instead. She *had* planted beads! She went very red.

'Why have you gone red?' said Mummy. 'Have you done something silly? You always go red then!'

Janet rushed out to the garden

19

without a word. She ran to her little plot. She began to scrape up the earth in which she had planted the beads – and sure enough, there they were, dirty, it is true, but still beads!

Janet began to cry. She had buried her nice glass beads in the dirt, and she still hadn't planted her poppy seeds, so John's would be out long before hers! What a silly she was!

John looked over the wall and saw Janet crying. 'What's the matter?' he said. 'Are you trying to water your garden with your tears, silly?'

'Oh, John – I've planted beads instead of seeds,' wept Janet. 'So, of course, they didn't grow, and now I am all behind with my seeds!'

'I'll help you to plant them,' said John, kindly, 'and we'll try and find the beads and wash them. What a stupid you are, Janet! You are always doing something like this!'

Well, they found all the beads they could, washed them and threaded them. There were not enough for a necklace, so it had to be a bracelet, and 'it looked quite pretty.

Then they planted the poppy seeds and covered them up. 'They'll soon grow,' said John. 'I'll give you the first poppy out of my garden, if you like – I've got a bud already.'

21

'Thank you, John,' said Janet, and went indoors. How Mummy and Auntie Laura laughed when they heard how she had planted beads instead of seeds!

'Little silly!' said Auntie. 'Did you think that if you planted beads they would grow up into necklaces? Well, well, well! You really must try and think harder another time.'

Perhaps Janet will. Her poppies aren't up yet, but she does hope they soon will be.

2

A Most Peculiar Bird

Peter and Betty were quarrelling. Mother heard them and frowned.

'Betty, you *must* have taken it!' said Peter. 'I left it here, by the window.'

'I did *not* take it!' said Betty. 'You always say I take your things, but I don't. It's you who take mine!'

'Oh, you fibber!' cried Peter. 'Now you just tell me where you've put my Red Indian hat or I'll smack all your dolls!'

'Peter, Peter!' called Mother. 'Don't talk like that. I expect your Red Indian hat is somewhere on the floor. It's very windy today and it must have blown off the window-sill and be somewhere by your bed.'

'It isn't, Mother. I've looked,' said Peter. 'Betty's been in my room, so she must have borrowed it. She knows I won't let her have it.'

'I *haven't* borrowed it!' cried Betty, in a temper. 'I haven't even *seen* the nasty horrid thing!'

'It isn't nasty and horrid,' said Peter. 'It's beautiful – heaps of coloured feathers that go round my head and hang down my back. It's the loveliest Indian head-dress that any boy in this town has got! Isn't it, Mother?'

Mother came into the room, 'I do wish you two would stop quarrelling,' she said. 'I don't expect Betty has taken it if she says she hasn't, Peter. Let *me* look for it. All this excitement about such a

silly little thing!'

Mother couldn't find it, but she was sure it would turn up. Things like that couldn't very well be lost. Betty looked sulkily at Peter and Peter looked sulkily back.

'I'm sure she's hidden it, horrid girl!' thought Peter and wouldn't play cards with her.

'I'm sure he thinks I've got it,' thought Betty and turned her back on Peter.

Well, after all that excitement in the morning, there was another excitement in the afternoon. Mother was sitting quietly sewing by the window when she heard the children shouting upstairs.

'Look at that! What can it be?'

'It's brilliant! It's some rare animal or bird!'

Mother wondered what the children were talking about. They came running to her in excitement.

'Mother! There's something up in the poplar tree! It's all colours. We think it must be a very rare bird!'

Mother was astonished. She looked out of the window at the poplar tree. She saw something very gay nearly at the top. She smiled a little smile.

'Dear me, it certainly looks like something rather surprising,' she said.

'Can we go out and see?' asked Peter. 'Mother, it may be a very, very rare bird; we ought to go and tell Mr. Kenny next door – the bird-man. He would be thrilled. He's always going out looking for birds, and writing about them.'

A Most Peculiar Bird

'Oh, I wouldn't bother him about it,' said Mother. But they did. They called over the wall to Mr. Kenny and told him.

'Mr. Kenny! There's a very rare bird up in our poplar tree. It's very brightly coloured – it may be a bird of paradise, or a parrot or a macaw! Perhaps it has lost its way and is tired and has come to roost in our tree.'

'Extraordinary!' said Mr. Kenny. 'I'll be along in a minute.'

In the greatest excitement the children ran to the poplar tree and peered up. 'It's got a very long tail!' said Betty.

'It's perfectly lovely,' said Peter. 'I wish I could see its head but I can't.'

'It doesn't seem to be making any noise at all – screeching or singing or whistling,' said Betty. 'It's quite still up there, Peter. Had we better get a ladder and climb up to it? If it's asleep we could catch it.'

So they got the ladder. Just as they set it up against the tree Mr. Kenny came

along. He stared in the greatest astonishment at the rare bird in the tree. Its
long feathery tail fluttered a little in the
strong wind.

'Amazing!' he said. 'Most astonishing.
What is it, I wonder? This is very
exciting.'

He pushed the children aside and
went up the ladder himself, very
cautiously so as not to frighten the
strange bird. The children held their
breath.

Nearer and nearer to the bird – nearer
and nearer. Mr. Kenny put out his hand
and touched the long, coloured tail. The
bird did not spread its wings and fly.
Mr. Kenny gave it a little tug. Still it did
nothing.

Then, to the children's surprise, Mr.
Kenny came down the ladder, jumped
off at the bottom and turned a disgusted
face to them.

'Silly children! A stupid trick! Wasting
my time like this. I'm ashamed of you!'

He strode away, leaving the children
puzzled and upset. Mr. Kenny had never

spoken to them like that before. 'He's left the bird up the tree,' said Peter.

'What's the matter with him? Why is he so cross?' said Betty. 'Peter, go up the ladder. I'll come just behind.'

So up they went and, like Mr. Kenny, Peter put out his hand to touch the bird's long, brilliant tail. He gave it a tug.

Something came tumbling down the tree. It wasn't a bird. It was – yes, of course, you've guessed – it was Peter's Red Indian head-dress! The wind had taken it off the window-sill that morning and blown it high up into the poplar tree! And there it had stayed until Peter had seen it that afternoon.

'Peter! It's your Red Indian hat!' cried Betty. 'And you said I'd taken it!'

Peter stared at it blowing in the wind.

'Sorry, Betty,' he said, his face red. 'Sorry, old thing!'

'It's all right,' said Betty, who was quick to forgive when anyone said they were sorry. 'But goodness, no wonder Mr. Kenny was cross. He must have thought we did it on purpose!'

They went to explain things to him. When he knew that the children had been taken in just as much as he had been, he laughed.

'Well, I did think it was a most peculiar bird!' he said. 'And it was the wind playing a joke on us all the time!'

'Yes – and Betty and I quarrelled like anything over the disappearance of the head-dress this morning!' said Peter. 'I'd better lend it to you, Betty, to wear – then we shall all know where it is!'

So for the first time Betty wore it – and she really does look fine!

3

A Hole in her Pocket

Jenny had a hole in her pocket. 'Bother!' she said. 'I believe my rubber has slipped through it!'

'Well, mend it, dear,' said her mother. 'You know how to mend a hole, surely!'

But Jenny couldn't be bothered. She wanted to go out and play. So out she went, and when she went to bed that night the hole was still in her pocket!

Now the next day her Uncle George came to see her mother – and he gave Jenny a bright new twenty pence. It shone so brightly that Jenny was sure it could only have been made the day before!

'I shall buy that tiny doll I saw in the toyshop window,' she said. 'I want her for my dolls' house. She's just the right size.'

But when she got to the toyshop, the money wasn't in her pocket! She felt for it – but all she found was the hole, just a little bit bigger now!

She ran home, crying, 'Oh, Mummy,

I've lost my bright new twenty pence. It was so beautiful. It's fallen through that hole in my pocket!'

'But I told you to mend it,' said Mummy. 'It's your own fault, Jenny.'

'I do have bad luck,' wept Jenny. 'I really do!'

'You bring your bad luck on yourself,' said Mummy. 'If you had mended the hole you wouldn't have had this bad luck! What about trying to bring a little good luck, and mending the hole now? You know what I always tell you – things go wrong if you yourself are silly, and they go right when you yourself try to do right.'

'I can't mend it,' wept Jenny. 'I've left my work-basket at school.'

'Then go and fetch it,' said Mummy. 'I've told you not to leave it there.'

Jenny dried her eyes. Perhaps she had better go and fetch it, though school was quite a long way off. She really must mend that hole! She set off, and Mummy was pleased.

'That's a good girl! I like it when you are sensible, and try to put things right, Jenny.'

Jenny got her little work-basket and set off home. She hadn't gone very far before she heard somebody crying. She ran to see who it was.

It was little Molly. She had tried to get some berries from the hedge, and had torn her frock badly. 'My mother will scold me!' she wept.

'Look – shall I mend the tear for you?' said Jenny. 'It just happens that I've got my little work-basket with me! Let me mend the tear. I can mend very neatly.'

Molly dried her eyes and watched Jenny sewing the hole up very neatly. 'Oh, how kind you are!' she said. 'Now my mother won't mind nearly so much. The hole hardly shows at all!'

A Hole in her Pocket

'There you are!' said Jenny, breaking off her thread. 'That's finished.'

Molly pressed a lovely red ball into Jenny's hands. 'Thank you!' she said. 'Take my ball, please, Jenny. It's just to show you how pleased I am!'

'But I've got plenty of balls,' said Jenny. 'No, you keep yours, Molly.'

Molly looked as if she was going to cry again. 'No, no, I want you to have it,' she said. 'You're so kind.'

So Jenny took it, and skipped off home again. But just round the corner she came across Johnny White looking up at a tree, and jumping up as high as he could.

'Somebody's thrown my new cap up there,' he said. 'Can you reach it, Jenny? I'll get in an awful row at school if I go without it.'

Jenny couldn't jump high enough to reach it either. But she had a very good idea. She took the ball that Molly had given to her and threw it at the cap. She missed it and the ball bounced down. She threw it again and it hit the cap, and down came both cap and ball!

'Goodness, you *are* clever!' said Johnny. 'Thank you most awfully, Jenny. Come and see my white mice, will you?'

She went in to see his white mice. He had some beauties. Jenny loved them. He suddenly picked one up and put it into her hand.

'You can have it,' he said. 'That's for getting my cap back for me.'

'Oh no – I don't want anything for that!' said Jenny. 'Really I don't!'

'Yes, take it,' said Johnny.

'Well – you have this ball in exchange then,' said Jenny. So Johnny took the ball and Jenny took the mouse. She popped the little thing into her work-basket and set off home again.

42

But she hadn't gone far before she remembered how afraid her mother was of mice! Gracious! It would never do to take it home. Her mother would be frightened and angry. Oh dear!

Jenny opened the work-basket and took a peep at the mouse. It put its little woffly nose up at her. It was sweet. A boy came to look, and he stroked the tiny thing.

'It's a beauty,' he said. 'I wish it was mine. I'll give you twenty pence for it! Will you sell it? It's the very nicest mouse I ever saw.'

'Yes, you can have it for twenty pence,' said Jenny, delighted. 'I love it, too, but I'm sure my mother won't let me keep it.'

The boy put his hand into his pocket and pulled out twenty pence. 'I found it today,' he said. 'Wasn't I lucky? It's very bright and shining and new.'

'Why – it's the one I lost out of the hole in my pocket!' cried Jenny, joyfully. 'It must be! It's so bright and new! Here, take the mouse. I'll run home and tell

Mummy all about it!'

She took the twenty pence and ran home. 'Mummy!' she called. 'I've got my twenty pence back!'

She told her mother all about it, and how Mummy laughed! 'Well, well, what a lot of happenings, all leading up to your twenty pence again. Now I suppose you'll be off to the toyshop to buy that little doll, after all!'

'Oh yes!' said Jenny, and she slipped the coin into her pocket – and it fell through the hole and rolled on to the floor!

'Oh,' she said and went very red. 'I *must* mend that hole first, mustn't I?'

And down she sat and mended it. 'If a thing's got to be done, it had better be done at once!' said Jenny. 'I shall lose my money again if I'm not careful!'

Wasn't she lucky to get it back?

4

Coltsfoot Magic

'I know a wonderful spell!' said Sly, the
gnome. 'One of the goblins who live
under the mountain told me!'

'What's the spell?' asked his sister,
Lightfoot.

'It's to make gold!' said Sly. 'I've
always wanted to do that. It's coltsfoot
magic. You know how golden the little
coltsfoot flower is – well, if you know the
right way, you can make a sack of gold
from a hundred flowering coltsfoot!'

'Well – what would you do with the
gold?' asked Lightfoot. 'Aren't you
happy enough in our pretty little
cottage, with me to cook for you and

46

look after you? What would you do with a lot of gold?'

'I'd buy the house at the end of the

village, the one with a view over the valley,' said Sly. 'I'd turn out Old Mother Slow. I don't like her! And I'd buy up all the best things in the market for myself. And I'd get a horse to ride, and wouldn't I just gallop about the countryside, making everyone get out of my way!'

'You're not liked very much now,' said Lightfoot, 'and I think you'd be liked even less then. You're not a nice enough person to be rich, Sly. Only good people should ever have money and power.'

'Don't be so rude,' said Sly, angrily.'I tell you this, Lightfoot - when I make my coltsfoot gold I'll turn you out and get someone who doesn't say impolite things to me, as you do! You can go and get someone who doesn't say impolite things to me, as you do! You can go and beg in the gutter for all I care.'

'You are unkind, Sly,' said Lightfoot. 'I am your sister, and I love you, even though you are often unkind and do wrong things. If you could make people happier by being rich then I would help you, But why should having money make you want to turn old Mother Slow

49

out of her home, and buy the best things in the market for yourself? No, no – I don't like this coltsfoot spell of yours!'

Sly went out angrily and slammed the door. He shouted for little Flighty, the goblin boy who dug his garden for him.

'Flighty! Come here! I've got a job for you to do. Go and pick me one hundred fine coltsfoot flowers – you know the ones I mean. They have round yellow heads a bit like dandelions, and scaly stalks.'

'But they're not yet out, sir,' said Flighty.

'Well, as soon as they spring up and flower, bring me one hundred, with their stalks and bring me one hundred of the leaves, too,' said Sly. 'I need the leaves for my spell, as well as the flowers.'

Lightfoot heard him giving Flighty his orders. She was sad. Now Sly would become rich, and he would be horrider than ever. He would make people unhappy. But how could she stop him? She went out to visit her friend, Dame Know-a-Lot. She told her all about it.

'Well, well, it's certainly a pity when people like your brother Sly get wealth and power,' said Dame Know-a-Lot. 'But I rather think, Lightfoot, that we can stop him making his spell!'

'How?' asked Lightfoot, surprised.

'Well, he says he wants the coltsfoot flowers *and* their leaves,' said Dame Know-a-Lot. 'I believe we could prevent the coltsfoot from sending up its leaves till the flowers are dead!'

51

'*Could* we? But how?' cried Lightfoot. 'I know all the moles that live about the countryside,' said Dame Know-a-Lot. 'And I could send them tunnelling underground to find all the hidden coltsfoot plants. They could tell them to send up their flowers first, but to hold down their leaves till the blossoms are over! Yes, I think I could manage it! No flower wants to be used for wrong purposes!'

'You do that, then,' said Lightfoot, pleased. 'I'm sure Sly wants the leaves as well as the flowers!'

He did, of course. He had to boil the flowers first in sunshine and water, and then add the leaves one by one, chanting magic words as he did so. Then he had to dance round in a circle whilst the mixture bubbled high. When it died down, every coltsfoot flower would have turned into a golden coin!

But when Flighty went to gather the coltsfoot flowers and leaves, he could find only flowers! Very puzzled indeed, he hunted everywhere – but no matter where he looked, he could find only flowers. Not one single coltsfoot leaf, with its cobwebby covering, could he find!

Sly was angry when Flighty came back with the flowers only.

'What use are they without leaves?' he stormed. 'I suppose I must seek them myself, you lazy, good-for-nothing scamp.'

He gave Flighty a cuff on the ear and

set off to hunt for coltsfoot leaves himself. But, of course, he couldn't find a single one either. It was most extraordinary!

Lightfoot didn't say a word when he

stormed and raved about it. She just went quietly about her work. Sly grew angrier and angrier.

'Don't you realise that if I can't get the leaves at the same time as the flowers, I can't possibly make that gold spell?' he shouted.

'It will be a good thing if you don't,' said Lightfoot. 'Now stop storming about, Sly, and come and have your dinner. You are lucky to have a nice meal. Don't spoil it by stamping about the room and letting it get cold.'

'I shall try and make the spell without the leaves,' said Sly, at last. 'I'll see what happens.'

'Now, Sly, you know it's dangerous to make a spell if you haven't got everything you need for it,' said Lightfoot. But Sly wouldn't listen to his sister. No - he began to make the coltsfoot spell without the leaves!

But, oh my goodness – it wasn't the same spell at all! To do the coltsfoot spell without leaves made a grow-small spell! Lightfoot, who was eating her dinner and watching, suddenly gave a loud cry.

'Sly! Sly! Stop the spell at once! Something is happening to you! You're growing smaller – and smaller! Stop, before it's too late!'

In a terrible fright, poor Sly stopped the spell. But he had dwindled to a quarter of his size, Now he was noly as big as a tall buttercup - and there was no way he knew of getting back to his right size again. What a state he was in!

'I'm sorry for you,Sly,' said Lightfoot. 'Now you are so small that even the children can smack you if they want to - and I'm sure they will, for you have often been unkind to them. What a pity you meddled with a gold spell!'

Poor Sly! He stayed small all his life, and he was always frightened of everything, because now even the dogs were bigger than he was! They came running after him, and sniffed at him in surprise, and he didn't like it at all.

'Better for him to be small and harmless than big and cruel,' thought Lightfoot. 'It's my fault he's gone small, because I meddled with the coltsfoot

flowers and their leaves – but he would have been such a horrid fellow if he had become rich!'

The curious thing is that to this day the coltsfoot flowers come up without their leaves! The leaves come much later. You watch and see!

5

The Bold Bad Boy

The children didn't at all like it when their cousin Tom came to stay. He was such a bold, bad boy!

He laughed at them for being afraid to do things. 'Pooh, can't climb to the top of a tree! Pooh, won't come and paddle in the pond! Won't come and chase the silly old cows!'

Alice, Sam and Peter were not afraid of doing any of those things. But they had just been forbidden to climb trees and paddle in the pond, and they knew it was wrong to chase the cows.

'We're not afraid. It's just that we're not allowed to do it!' said Alice. 'You're a bold, bad boy, always wanting to get us into trouble.'

'You're babies,' said Tom. 'I wish I

hadn't got babies for cousins. Look how Alice screams when I hide behind a door and jump at her.'

'It's a horrid trick!' said Alice. 'I hate the way you're always trying to frighten us and make us jump. You know Sam is only five. You made him dreadfully frightened last night when you hid under his bed and growled and pulled all his bedclothes off. He thought you were a bear.'

Tom laughed. 'Sam shouldn't be such a coward,' he said.

'He's not,' said Peter. 'He didn't cry or squeal out. He was very, very brave.'

Tom really was a most unpleasant boy. When he found out that his three cousins really did hate to be jumped at, and scared, he did it all the more! They got very tired of it, and at last they thought they would try and give *him* a fright.

Tom slept alone at night in a little room. The three children made their plans carefully.

'I'll be the Whistling Owl,' said Alice.

'Sam, you can be the Popping Panda. And Peter, you can be the Windy Willies.'

The two boys stared at her. 'What's a Whistling Owl?' asked Peter. 'I've never heard of that kind of owl.'

'Nor have I, really,' said Alice, with a giggle. 'I just made up all the names. The Whistling Owl is a creature that makes a dreadful squeaking noise. I'm going to hide behind Tom's window curtains when he's in bed, and rub my wetted finger up and down the pane. You know what a squeaking noise that makes!'

'How can I be a Popping Panda?' asked Sam.

'The Popping Panda keeps going Bang!' said Alice. 'I'll give you a whole lot of paper bags I've saved up and you can keep blowing them up and bursting them. They will make a lovely POP for the Popping Panda!'

'And what about me?' said Peter, looking thrilled. 'How shall I be the Windy Willies?'

The Bold Bad Boy

'I'll give you the bellows out of the dining room,' said Alice. 'You can keep blowing air in and out of them over Tom's bed, and you can make a groaning noise, too, if you like.'

'It all sounds very funny,' said Peter. 'It will serve Tom right for frightening us as he does. When he finds out what it's like to be scared maybe he won't think it's funny after all.'

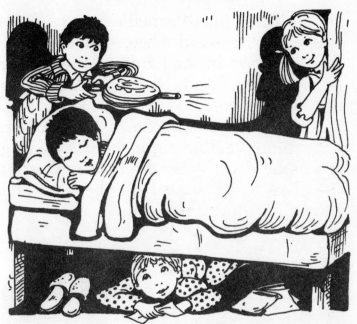

That night, when Tom was safely in bed and asleep, the three children crept into his room. Alice got behind the window curtains. Sam got under the bed with his paper bags. Peter got behind the head of the bed with the bellows.

Now, Tom had heard about the Whistling Owl, the Popping Panda and the Windy Willies. Alice had talked about them loudly with the other two, and Tom had listened scornfully.

'What are all these silly things?' he said. 'Do you say they've escaped from a circus or something? I don't believe in any of them! It's just like you three to be scared of them!'

He was asleep when the children crept into his room. Alice began the fun by rubbing her finger up and down the window-pane.

'Eeeeeeeeeeee!'

Tom woke up with a jump. 'Eeeeeeee!' Alice made the squeaking noise again. Then Sam, under the bed, blew up a paper bag and burst it with a loud POP!

Peter, trying not to giggle, worked the bellows hard, and a cold draught blew Tom's hair straight over his face!

'Oooh!' said Tom. 'Ow!'

'Eeeeeeeeee!' went Alice's finger, rubbing up and down the window-pane. 'BANG! POP! BANG!' went Sam's bags under the bed. 'Whoooosh!' went Peter's bellows, blowing cold air down Tom's neck.

'It's the Whistling Owl – and the Popping Panda! And the Windy Willies!' yelled Tom, scared and trembling. 'Oh, what shall I do? They've all escaped and got into my room. Oooooooo!'

'Eeeeeeeeeee! POP! Whooooooosh!'

'Help me, save me!' yelled Tom at the

top of his voice. 'Alice, Sam, Peter! Come and save me!'

The three children made their way quietly to the door, and Peter put his bellows outside there. Then they all trooped in, in the darkness, saying: 'What's the matter, Tom? Why are you calling us?'

'Look out! The Whistling Owl's here, and the Popping Panda, and the Windy Willies!' called Tom.

'At them, boys, at them!' cried Alice, and she and Sam and Peter pretended to hit and bang all the place, still in the dark. Tom hid his head under the clothes. He was sobbing.

Suddenly the light was switched on, and there was Mother, looking most astonished. 'What's all this?' she said sternly. Tom peeped out.

71

'Oh, Aunt Joan, don't scold the others!' he begged. 'They're terribly, terribly brave! I was attacked by a Whistling Owl, a Popping Panda and the Windy Willies –and they came and fought them and sent them away!'

'Hmmmmmmm,' said Mother, and she looked at her three children.

'Tom's always jumping out at us and laughing because we get scared,' said Alice. 'It's funny, Mother, isn't it, that he got so scared of an owl, a panda and a willy? We *soon* sent them away.'

'Hmmmm!' said Mother again, remembering the pair of bellows she had seen outside the door. 'Well, get back to bed now. Tom, now that you know what it's like to feel so scared, I wouldn't try and frighten other people any more.'

'Because you never know when the Whistling Owl, the Popping Panda and the Windy Willies might come back!' giggled Alice.

Tom began to think he had been tricked, and he felt ashamed of his cries and sobs. But, oh dear, when he remembered the squeaking 'Eeeeeeee!' the loud POP and the whoosh of the cold wind on his neck he got scared again. And he crept into bed with Sam and Peter in the next room! How they laughed!

'I guess you won't jump out and boo at us any more,' said Peter. And he was right. Tom didn't. Wasn't it a funny trick the others played on him?

6

Surprise for Mother and Susan

On the bookcase was a round glass bowl full of water. In it, swimming about in some strands of green water-weed, was a fine goldfish.

He belonged to Susan. She loved Goldie. She fed him, saw that he had some nice weed in his globe all the time, and once she gave him two water-snails for company. But they ate his weed so she took them out.

Goldie wasn't at all lonely. He liked talking to the toys, when the nursery was empty. They all liked Goldie, too. He swam round and round his bowl, and sometimes he poked his nose right out of the water.

'I do wish you'd come right out and play with us!' said the sailor doll. 'Why

don't you?'

'Well, I have to live in water,' said Goldie. 'I'd like to come and play with you, really I would – but, after all, I've no legs or arms, so I wouldn't be much fun.'

'You could slither along on the floor,' said the sailor doll. 'Do come.'

But Goldie wouldn't. He didn't mind poking his nose out of the water now and again, but he didn't think he would like to get right out.

'Susan's got a toy goldfish that swims in her bath at night,' the panda told Goldie one day. 'Susan puts him in when the bath is full and takes him out again when it's empty. He lies there in the soap-rack all day and he doesn't seem to mind. If he can live out of the water, why can't you?'

'I don't know. I just don't want to get out of my bowl,' said Goldie, rather crossly.

'He's just silly,' said the sailor doll, getting cross himself. 'He won't try!'

Now when the sailor doll made up his mind that he wanted something, he went on and on until he got what he wanted! And he suddenly made up his mind he wanted Goldie to get out of his bowl. But how could he make him?

He thought of an idea at last. 'I'll get the toys to have some sports,' he thought. 'Yes – running and jumping, for prizes. I'll offer the prizes. I've got a sweet hidden at the back of the cupboard. And there's a bit of red ribbon I found in the waste-paper basket. That will do for another prize.'

The toys were quite excited when they heard about the sports. The panda helped the sailor doll to arrange them. The toys had to run round the nursery to race one another. They had to see how high they could jump over a rope. And they had to choose partners for a three-legged race, too.

'I'll give a prize for that,' said the panda. 'I've got a brooch out of a cracker. I'll offer that as a prize for the three-legged race.'

'Goldie ought to go in for the sports,

too,' said the sailor doll.

'Don't be silly,' said the panda. 'He can't run. And how could he possibly go in for the three-legged race when he hasn't got even one leg?'

'But he could jump,' said the sailor doll. 'He could jump high out of the water. He could jump right out of his bowl! We could easily put him back. If we thought he had jumped the best, we could give him the prize. He would look nice with the red ribbon round his neck.'

Goldie couldn't help feeling rather excited when he heard all this. He pressed his nose against the glass of his bowl, and tried to see all that was going on.

The sailor doll climbed up on the bookcase. 'Do you want to go in for the jumping prize?' he asked Goldie. 'I bet you could win it! I once saw you jump a little way out of your water, and it was a very good jump. Don't you want a red ribbon?'

'Well – I'll go in for the jumping,' said Goldie. 'Yes, I will! You tell me when it's

80

my turn.'

The sports were to be held that night.
The toys were excited. They started off
with the running race and the toy rabbit
easily won that. He simply galloped
round and came to the winning-post
long before the others. He was very
pleased with the sweet for a prize. It was
a bit old and dirty, but he didn't mind.

'Now for the jumping,' said the sailor doll. 'And let me tell you, toys, that the goldfish is going in for this, too! My word, I guess he'll jump high!'

All the toys took their turn at jumping. The kangaroo out of the Noah's Ark jumped the highest of all. Goldie popped his head out of the water.

'I can jump higher than the kangaroo – I can, I can!' he called, in his bubbling voice. 'Watch me!'

He jumped high out of the water – very high indeed! But alas, when he fell back, he struck the edge of the bowl, and bounced over on to the bookcase, instead of back into the water.

He slithered from the bookcase, and

fell over to the edge. Thud! He crashed to the floor, and lay there wriggling and gasping.

'I can't breathe!' he gasped. 'I can't breathe out of water. Put me back, quickly, or I shall die.'

The toys were horrified. The panda rushed to him, but he couldn't get hold of Goldie, he was so slippery. And even if he could hold him, how could he possibly get him back up to the top of the bookcase?

Goldie wriggled hard on the carpet. 'Water, water!' he gasped. 'I'm dying! Water, get me water!'

'Sailor doll! Tell us what to do. *You* made poor Goldie jump!' cried the toys.

The sailor doll was almost crying. He had got his way. He had made Goldie jump out of his bowl. Now he wanted nothing better than to get the poor goldfish back into his water. How could he have been so stupid and unkind as to try and make him jump out?

'Go on, sailor doll, do something!' shouted the toys. 'It's your fault, it's your fault!'

'I can't climb up the bookcase with Goldie, I can't,' sobbed the sailor doll. 'He's too heavy and too slippery.'

'I know what you can do! I know!'
squeaked the rabbit. 'Look, there is a
bowl of flowers on the table, You can
climb up the chair, surely , and then on
the table. Quick, pick Goldie up in your
arms, and climb up. Quick, quick! He's
almost dead!'

The poor goldfish was hardly wriggling at all now. He lay on the carpet,
gasping, his mouth opening and shutting feebly. The toys couldn't bear to see
him like that.

The sailor doll picked him up. he was
wet and slippery and heavy. The sailor
managed to climb up on to the chair
seat with him, with the toys helping
him. Then up on to the table he went,
panting and sobbing. He ran to the
flower bowl. It was a deep green bowl
and Mother had put some green sprays
in it, for there were few flowers out so
early in the year.

The sailor doll flung the goldfish into
the bowl of greenery. He slid down into
the water. At once he felt better, He
wriggled feebly at first, taking in great

gulps of water, and then felt stronger.
The toys all climbed up on the table to
watch. They saw Goldie flap his tail and
fins rather feebly. Then they saw him
wriggle himself – and then they saw
him try to swim, opening and shutting
his mouth as he always did.

'Goldie, dear Goldie, are you all right now?' asked Panda. 'Do you feel better?'

'Yes, Much better,' said Goldie, coming to the top of the water and poking his nose out between the stems. 'But I do think it was mean of the sailor doll to make me go in for the jumping, He might have known I would fall out and crash down to the floor.'

'I wanted you to fall out, I wanted you to come and play with us,' said the sailor doll, wiping his tears away, 'I thought if only I could make you jump out, you'd be quite all right, and could come and join our games. I didn't know you would die out of water.'

'Now I'm in a pretty fix,' said Goldie. 'All mixed up with these stems. And the water doesn't taste very nice either. Panda, did I jump high? I haven't even got a prize.'

'You shall have the red ribbon,' said the sailor doll at once. 'Come up to the top and I'll tie it round your neck. You really do deserve it, Goldie. Nobody jumped so far as you - right out of the bowl and down to the floor! Gracious, no one else would dare to jump off the bookcase.'

Goldie couldn't help feeling pleased to have the prize ribbon round his neck. He felt very grand and important. He swam in and out of the stems, looking very fine.

The toys went back to the toy cupboard. The night went and the morning came. And in the morning Susan ran into the nursery. She looked at the goldfish's bowl as she always did - and stared in astonishment.

'It's empty!' she cried. 'Where's

Goldie? Oh - surely he hasn't jumped out and died.'

But he was nowhere on the floor - nowhere to be found at all! Susan ran to tell her mother. Together they hunted about for Goldie. But they couldn't find him.

'Well, lay the breakfast, dear,' said Mother at last. 'Goldie's gone. Goodness knows where to!'

Susan laid the breakfast, feeling very sad. She and her mother sat down - and then her mother gave a cry of surprise.

'Susan! Look, Goldie's in the flower bowl! How *did* he get there? Did you put him there?'

'Oh, Mummy, *no!* Of course not!' said Susan, in astonishment. 'I've been very miserable about him. Mummy, he *is* in the flower bowl - he's swimming about among the stems!'

Mother and Susan watched Goldie in amazement - and then Susan saw the ribbon round his neck. It was very limp and wet, of course – but still, it was a ribbon.

'Oh Sue – you *must* have put the ribbon round his neck and popped him into the flower bowl to give me a surprise!' said Mother. And she simply wouldn't believe that Susan hadn't done it.

But Susan knew she hadn't. She looked round at her toys, and she saw that the sailor-doll was wet all down the front of him. He winked at her.

'It's something to do with the sailor-doll,' thought Susan. 'It is, it is! But what? If only he could talk to me. Now, I'll never know what happened!'

You can tell her if you ever meet her. But I'm not sure she'll believe you. Wasn't it a surprise for Susan and her mother?

7

I Dare You To!

It was very cold weather. There was thick ice on the puddles. The village pond was frozen hard, and the ducks couldn't think what had happened to it.

'Can't we slide on the pond yet?' said Tom. His school-teacher looked up.

'Not till I put the notice up,' he said. 'It isn't quite safe yet. Another night or two of frost and it will be all right. The ice isn't quite thick enough.'

'But, sir – we saw a couple of boys from the next village on it today,' said John. 'It seemed to be bearing all right.'

'I've nothing to do with the boys in the next village,' said the master. 'I'm in charge of *you* – and I'm not running any risks of any of you falling in and drowning. I went on it myself this morning, and I heard it crack as I walked.'

The boys grumbled. Surely the ice was thick enough! Why, some of the big puddles were frozen solid – surely the ice on the pond must be almost solid, too! The teacher couldn't have heard it crack that morning!

The boys all went home after school that day. They passed the pond on their way and looked at it longingly. Oh, for a slide on it! It was such a nice big pond. You could have a very fine slide indeed. Soon there would be skating.

'My uncle's given me a fine pair of skates,' said Tom. 'I shall go skating on Saturday – if only Mr. Brown doesn't still think he hears the ice cracking!'

'I've got a toboggan,' said John. 'If there is snow on the hills, I shall go sledging. I shall have some fun, I can tell you!'

'My father's going to teach me how to skate properly,' said Tom. 'You'll soon see me gliding up and down at sixty miles an hour!'

I Dare You To!

'My mother's told me I can fetch my cousins on Saturday. They've got toboggans, too,' said John. 'They will all come home to tea with me afterwards. My, we'll have some fun!'

The two boys tapped the edge of the pond with their toes. It felt thick and solid. How they wished they could have just one slide! The other boys watched them tapping the ice with their toes and they tapped too.

'I say - look - there are the two big boys from the next village again!' said Tom, suddenly. 'Look - they're going on the ice!'

The two boys ran on the ice and began to slide up and down, up and down. The other boys watched them enviously.

'Hi! You know it's not supposed to be safe yet, don't you?' yelled Tom.

The boys slid up to them. 'What's not safe?' said one of them. 'Your pond? Pooh! It's as safe as can be. The ice is inches thick! Aren't you boys coming on for a slide?'

'No,' said Tom. 'We've been told it's not safe yet. We've got to wait.'

'Babies! Cowards!' said the boy, sliding off again. 'You're afraid, that's what's the matter with you! Cowardy-cowardy-custard!'

'We're jolly well not afraid!' yelled John, angrily. 'It's like your cheek to say that – coming from another village and sliding on *our* pond! You wait till we're allowed on. We'll soon chase you off!'

'Come on and chase us off now!' mocked the two boys, sliding about. 'Come on!'

One of them slid near to Tom and John. 'I dare you to come on the ice!' he shouted. 'I dare you to!'

Tom and John hesitated.

'Babies! You're scared! I dare you to come!' yelled the boy.

'We can't be thought cowards, can we?' cried Tom, and he slid on to the ice. John followed. The two boys yelled rude things at them.

'Come on. After them!' shouted Tom.

'We'll show them if we're afraid or not! I always do what I'm dared to do!'

The other two boys set off to the farther end of the pond. Tom and John followed them, close together. But just as they got to the middle, a horrible noise sounded.

'Crack-crack-crack-crack!'

It was the ice cracking. The weight of the two boys close together had been too much for it, for there was a thin place just there. An enormous crack had come, which widened quickly. Icy-blue water showed.

Tom was sliding and couldn't stop himself. He slid right into the crack, and fell into the water. Poor John followed him. They yelled as the cold water crept up to their waists.

'Help! Save us! Help!' they yelled in fright. They clutched at the cold edge of the cracked ice, but it was so cold and slippery that they could not hold it.

The two boys from the next village took fright and fled away. The boys, Tom's friends and John's stared with

frightened eyes.

'Fetch help!' yelled Tom. 'Quick! We'll drown!'

One of the boys darted off. He raced to the nearest house. There he found a sensible woman, who, carrying a long ladder, came as quickly as she could to the pond. She laid the ladder down flat on the ice, and it reached the two boys.

'Get hold! Clamber up!' she shouted. Tom managed to clutch the last rung. He turned and pulled John there, too. The two boys were so icy-cold that they could hardly use their hands.

But soon they were trying to clamber along the ladder that was lying flat over the icy pond. They reached the woman and she pulled them quickly to the bank.

'Silly boys! Going on the ice before it was fit to bear!' she scolded.

'You'll catch your deaths of cold. Where do you live?'

'Not far off,' said Tom, whose teeth were chattering so much that he could hardly speak. 'We can run to our homes, both of us. Th-th-th-thank you for your h-h-h-help!'

Shivering with the cold, the two boys got to their homes as quickly as they could. Their mothers were shocked to see them so wet and so cold. Quickly they stripped off their dripping things, and bundled them into warm beds and gave them hot drinks.

But it was too late. The next day both Tom and John had terrible colds and coughs. They felt very ill. They didn't want anything to eat.

They were ill for three weeks. During that time the pond froze very hard, and people skated and slid all day long. The snow covered the hills too, and everyone went sledging and snowballing. The boys and girls at the village school had a wonderful time.

When Tom and John were better at last, and able to go back to school, the snow had melted and the pond was water again, with ducks swimming gaily on it. The cold weather had gone for good – and the two boys had missed

104

it all. How upset they were!

Their schoolmaster welcomed them back, but he didn't seem at all sorry for them when they grumbled that the cold weather had gone.

'You deserve to miss it,' he said. 'You were very disobedient.'

'Sir - we didn't mean to be,' said Tom.

'We were going to obey you, really we were - but the two boys from the next village called us cowards for not going on the pond.'

'Yes, sir - and they dared us to!' said John. 'They said "We dare you to. Come on - we dare you to."'

'So we just had to go on, you see, sir,' said Tom. 'If they dared us, what else could we do? We had to be brave and show it.'

'Now look here,' said Mr. Brown, 'let's get this silly "daring" business right. You were going to be loyal and obedient to my wishes - but someone else, that you don't know and don't care tuppence about, comes along and says "I dare you to" - and you throw away all your loyalty and common sense, and do what they dare you to do, simply becaue you are afraid they will think you're cowards!'

The two boys looked at him. He went on, speaking in his low, even voice.

106

'You were so afraid they would think you afraid, that you let your fear of their scorn conquer you, and you did the silliest thing you could do – went on to a pond that didn't bear. Not very daring, Tom and John. The *really* brave thing would have been to say, "Think us cowards if you like – but we've promised not to go on, and we're not afraid of keeping our promise!"'

'Yes,' said Tom, suddenly seeing that Mr. Brown was quite right. 'The thing we thought was brave, wasn't. It was just silly, done because we were dared to do it. The really brave thing would have been to laugh – and not to go out on the ice. I see, sir.'

'Good!' said his master. 'Three weeks in bed will be worth it, if you see the difference between a silly "dare", and loyalty to a promise. Well – I hope we get some cold weather again and we can send you off to slide and toboggan after all.'

But the cold weather didn't come again that year. It was a pity, because now the two boys will have to wait till next winter!

8

Two Little Meddlers

There were once two children who couldn't keep their fingers out of anything.

'Meddling here and meddling there!' their mother said, crossly. 'Fiddling in my work-basket and muddling up my needlework. Dropping the needles out of my knitting! Keep your hands to yourselves, Tessie and Will!'

'Who's been meddling in my shed?' the gardener said. 'Upsetting the whitewash! Tangling up the raffia! Mixing the soot and lime! Wait till I catch them!'

'Who's been in my kitchen?' said the cook. 'Look at those taps left running! And who's broken that plate? Tessie and Will, I'll be bound! Little meddlers!'

They really *were* meddlers. They had to fidget with everything, pick up everything, hold it, see what it could do.

They simply wouldn't keep their hands to themselves.

I expect you know children like that and hate them to come to tea with you, because they will want to meddle with your precious stamp-book, or overwind your engine, or make a hole in your doll to see what's inside her. You can't stop them!

Now one day Tessie and Will took the bus to go to Heyho Hill. That was where their aunt lived, and they knew it well.

'I'll get rid of you for one day at least!' said their mother. '*One* of you has meddled with my sewing-machine and I really must get it put right today. So off you go to Auntie Polly – and remember, she *smacks* meddling hands! She's much harder-hearted than I am and smacks really hard!'

So off went Tessie and Will to Auntie Polly. But, when they were in the bus, they began to meddle with the windows, to find out how they opened and shut. And they were so interested in their meddling that they went right past Heyho Hill.

'Gracious! We've gone too far!' said Tessie. 'Come on, Will, we'd better get out here.'

So out they got and began to walk back. They thought they would take a short cut, though they were not really sure of the way. They cut across a field and came to a little blue shed set by a stream. A noise came from the shed, and they wondered what it was.

'It sounds like bubbling and gurgling

and boiling and humming and hissing,' said Tessie. 'What can it be?'

'Let's go in and see,' said Will. So they knocked on the door. There was no answer at all. Only the bubbling and gurgling went on as before, sounding more mysterious then ever.

'Let's go in,' said Tessie, and she pushed open the door. It swung to with a loud slam behind her and Will. The children stood still in amazement and wonder.

They were in a very ling, wide shed, the biggest shed they had ever seen.But how could that be, because from the outside it hadn't looked much bigger than a bicycle shed?

All round the sides of the shed were bowls and wheels and pipes and whirring belts. Some of the bowls held queer liquids that bubbled and hissed, sending up streams of coloured smoke. The wheels ran round and round with long belts on them, and they hummed and roared.

The pipes puffed and panted and gurgled. All kinds of brightly-coloured taps were here and there, and one of them was dripping a bright blue drop, as blue as the sky.

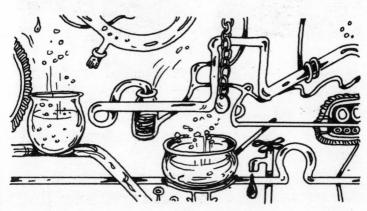

The funny thing was – there was nobody there, nobody at all! The pipes and wheels and belts and bowls worked away as fast as possible, all making their different noises, but nobody was there to watch them or work at them. How very queer!

'Let's go,' said Tessie. 'It's so odd, all this! What can it be? Let's go!'

They tried to open the door – but they couldn't! It was jammed so tight that they couldn't move it an inch.

They stared again at all the taps and wheels and pipes. 'I wonder what happens when you turn on *this* tap,' said Tessie, and she turned on a bright golden tap just near her.

A stream of brilliant green water rushed out, bubbling and gurgling. It was hot and full of queer bubbles that rose into the air from it, bumping into one another without breaking.

'Oooh – aren't they pretty?' said Tessie. 'Turn on another tap, Will, and see what happens.'

Will turned on a bright silver tap. But no bubbly liquid came from it, only something that looked like strings upon strings of blue toffee! It unwound itself slowly from the tap, like a toffee snake!

'Gracious, look at that!' cried Tessie. 'Isn't this an exciting place, Will? You'd better turn off that tap.'

'I can't,' said Will, trying. 'It's like the door, it seems to have got jammed!'

'What's in this bowl?' said Tessie, and she peered into a deep bowl which seemed to hold only darkness. There was a long-handled spoon nearby. She stirred the darkness in the bowl with the spoon.

Such a mournful howl came up from the bowl that she jumped. Some of the darkness splashed up at her and dripped on to her frock. The little dark spot it made howled too, just like a dog in fear.

'Oh!' said Tessie, startled. 'This drip on my frock is making such a funny noise, Will. Can you wipe it off?'

But it wouldn't be wiped off, so wherever Tessie moved in the shed the little moaning noise went with her. It was a nuisance.

'This wheel has stopped turning; I wonder why,' said Will, and he gave the wheel a turn with his hand. It began to spin round and round. It spun faster and faster and faster, then suddenly it burst with a loud noise, and sharp little pieces flew all over the children. They fell over with the shock, and stared at the place where the wheel had been.

'Oooh,' said Tessie, scared. 'Perhaps we oughtn't to have touched it. It spun so fast that it spun itself to bits.'

Tessie's eye caught sight of a rope. It was deep yellow, set with bright little bead-like things that winked in the sunlight. It swung slowly to and fro.

'What's that rope for?' she said, getting up. 'I'll pull it and see what happens.'

She tugged at it – and down from the ceiling came a shower of bright blue water! It fell over both children and

117

soaked them to the skin.

'Oh!' said Will, shaking himself. 'Why did you touch that rope, you stupid thing? Now look at us! Why, we're dyed blue! Whatever shall we do about it?'

So they were. Their skins were a bright blue! The little spot of darkness on Tessie's dress didn't seem to like it and began to moan more loudly.

'I wish this silly spot would stop making a noise!' said Tessie, and tried to wipe it away again with her blue hand. She was all blue now, dress and shoes and all! Even her hair was blue!

Now you might have thought that the two silly meddlers had had enough of meddling, wouldn't you? But meddlers simply can't stop, you know. So when Will saw a big bath of what looked like gold dust, he was full of curiosity.

'Look, Tessie,' he said. 'What's this gold dust in here? See how it shines. Do you think it really *is* gold dust?'

Tessie looked. It certainly did shine beautifully! She saw a handle at the side of the big bath and pulled it.

At once the gold dust shot out from the bath all over the two children. It went into their mouths and up their noses, and into their hair and over every inch of their bodies, right through their blue clothes! Well, well, well!

They began to cough - and out of their mouths came the dust. But it wasn't bright gold anymore, it was just ordinary dust. They hadn't noticed that the sunlight had lain on the dust and made it golden.

They coughed and they coughed. They shivered in their soaked clothes. They didn't like the smell of the blue dye. And all the time the little spot of darkness kept whining as if it was a live thing.

Tessie wished she had had some scissors in her pocket, then she would have cut it out!

Suddenly the door of the shed opened, and someone came in. What a queer person! Tessie and Will knew at once that he was an enchanter. They had seen pictures of enchanters in their books. This one had a flying cloak of silver and blue, a tall pointed hat of black, and shoes that turned up at the toes in a very curious way. His beard reached down to the floor.

He had eyes that seemed to go right through Tessie and Will. He frowned and it was a fearful frown. He looked all round and saw the green water running away out of the first tap, and the blue toffee out of the second tap. There was a dreadful mess on the floor.

'Why have you come meddling here?' he asked, in a voice that sounded like far-away thunder. 'Meddlers! Interferers! Can't keep your hands to yourself or your noses out of things that are nothing to do with you. Go, before I make you my servants!'

'Oh, but, please, we can't go home like

121

this!' said Tessie. 'Look, we're blue all over – and we're soaking wet – and we're full of dust. It's down our throats and everywhere.'

She coughed and sneezed. The enchanter suddenly smiled. 'Ah, I can put you right,' he said. 'That is, if you wish it.'

'Oh, yes we do, we do,' said Will. The enchanter clapped his hands and a door appeared at the other end of the long shed.

'Go through there,' he said. 'You will find some of my servants and they will see that you are dried, scrubbed, and that the dust is well shaken out of you.'

The children ran through the door. On the other side was yet another vast shed, with more machinery in it. Little brown men were running about busily. As soon as they saw the children they ran up to them.

'You want to be scrubbed free of the blue dye!' they said, and popped the children in a big bath. Great scrubbing-brushes came down from the roof and

began to scrub them. How they
scrubbed! Tessie and Will yelled and
tried to get out of the bath, but it wasn't
a bit of good. They had to stay and be
scrubbed till every speck of blue had
gone.

'Now to squeeze you dry!' said the
little brownies, and hurried them to
what looked like a big mangle. In went
the children, and, oh dear, they were
nearly squeezed to bits and every scrap
of breath went out of them!

Plop! They came out the other side of the mangle, feeling very thin and breathless. But they soon got back their right shape.

'And now to get the dust off you!' cried the brownies, and took up little carpet-beaters. They stood in a ring round the children and began to slap them hard with the flat little beaters. Biff, biff, bang, bang, slap, slap!

'Oh, don't hit so hard! Oh, you're whipping us!' cried Will, and tried to skip out of the way. But he couldn't. The brownies went on beating the dust out of them in clouds, till at last, sore and bruised, the children stood without a speck of dust in them anywhere.

'There you are. You're all right now. You can go,' said the brownies, and made another door come nearby. Tessie and Will flew out as fast as they could. They were crying.

'I wish we'd never gone into that shed! I wish we'd never meddled!' wept Tessie. 'Oh, how sore I am with that scrubbing and squeezing and beating! I'll never meddle again, never!'

Well, of course, it's easy to say you'll get out of a bad habit, but difficult to keep your word. And that's just what

Tessie and Will found. But they also found something else, and this is very queer.

You remember that spot of darkness that made a peculiar noise? Well, it's gone from her dress, but it must be somewhere about poor Tessie, because as soon as she starts to meddle, she hears that moaning noise again.

And as soon as Will begins to fiddle with something he shouldn't touch, his fingernails turn blue again, and he stops at once.

They never meddle when I'm about, but I sometimes wish they would, because I'd like to hear that funny noise and see Will's fingernails turn blue. Wouldn't you? But if ever I find myself in that strange shed down by the stream, I'm going to be *very, very* careful!

9

The Swallow Fairy

Once there was a small fairy who played all summer long with the swallows. She had long curved wings as they had, and she flashed in the air with them, racing them over the fields and back.

They lived on the insects they caught in the air. The swallow fairy lived on the honey she found in the flowers. The bees and butterflies showed her how to get it with a long, very tiny spoon.

'We have a tongue to put into the flowers, to suck out the honey,' they said, 'but you haven't a long enough one. So use a spoon.'

Now, in October, a cold wind blew. The swallow fairy shivered. There were not so many flowers with honey in and

she was sometimes hungry.

There were not so many insects flying in the air, either, so the swallows were often hungry. And when the cold wind blew, they gathered together on the roofs of the barns and on the telegraph wires, chattering and twittering.

The little martins were there with the swallows, too. They were cousins of the swallows, and loved to fly with them high in the sky. 'Don't let's stay here in this cold wind!' they cried. 'Let's fly off to a warmer country.'

'Yes, do let's!' said the swallows. 'In a warmer country there will be more insects. There are so few here now. We will go!'

'Oh, don't leave me!' cried the swallow fairy. 'I shall be so lonely. Take me with you.'

'It's too far for you to fly,' said her best friend, a fine long-tailed swallow with a shining steel-blue back. 'You would fall into the sea and be drowned.'

'Oh, will you fly across the sea?' said the fairy. 'I shouldn't like that. I'll stay

here – but will you come back again?'

'In the springtime,' said the swallow, and then suddenly, almost as if one of them had given a signal, the whole

twittering flock flew into the air and wheeled away to the south. They were gone. Not one was left.

The fairy was lonely. She sat crying in the evening wind, sitting on a barn roof by herself. A little black bat saw her and flew near.

'Come and live with me!' he cried. 'Do come!' So the fairy went to live with him. But as the wind grew colder he wouldn't go out to fly. He hung himself upside down in an old cave, with hundreds of others like himself. And he went to sleep!

'Wake up, wake up!' cried the fairy. 'You're a dull sort of friend to have, little bat!'

'Leave me alone,' said the bat, sleepily. 'I'm too cold to fly. I shall sleep till the sun comes again in the spring. Hang yourself upside down, fairy, and sleep too.'

'I don't like hanging upside down,' said the fairy. 'I don't like hanging myself up at all. And I don't like this cave, either. It smells.'

'Well, go and live with someone else then,' said the bat, in a huff, and wouldn't say another word.

The fairy flew off. She came to a pond and sat by it, feeling cold and lonely. A frog was there, talking to a fat, squat toad. 'Hallo, fairy!' said the frog. 'Why do you look so miserable?'

'I'm lonely,' said the fairy. 'I've no friend to live with.'

'You'd better tuck yourself away somewhere for the winter,' said the frog. 'Come with me and I'll keep you close to me, little fairy.'

'All right,' said the fairy. 'Where are you going?'

'I'm going down into the mud at the bottom of the pond,' said the frog. 'I shall sleep there all winter. It's a nice cosy place to sleep.'

'Oh, I'd *hate* that!' said the fairy and shivered. 'Cold and muddy and wet! I'd rather go with the toad. I always did like his lovely brown eyes.'

'Yes, you come with me,' said the toad, and took her to a big stone. Underneath was a fine hiding-place, just big enough for the fairy and himself. He dragged her underneath with him. Then he shut his eyes. The fairy went to sleep, too. But she soon awoke and shivered.

'This is a nasty damp place,' she said. 'I shall get a cold. Toad, let's go somewhere else.'

But the toad was fast asleep and wouldn't answer. So the fairy left him in disgust. She walked fast to keep herself

warm - and she ran into a hedgehog,
also hurrying fast. He carried a leaf in
his mouth.'

'Oh, hullo!'said the fairy. 'Where are
you off to, with that leaf?'

'I've got a cosy little house in a warm
bank,' said the hedgehog. 'I'm lining it
with leaves. Why don't you come and
live with me there? It's really a very nice
little home, with a curtain of moss for a
door.'

'All right, I'll come,' said the fairy,

who thought the hedgehog's home sounded nice, too, all lined with dry dead leaves, and quite warm.

But the hedgehog was so prickly that the fairy couldn't possibly cuddle up to him. And whenever he moved, his prickles stuck into her. That wasn't at all nice.

'I'll have to go,' said the fairy. 'I'm sorry, but you're not very cuddly, hedgehog.'

The hedgehog said nothing. He was fast asleep. He wouldn't wake up for weeks!

'This is very boring,' said the fairy to herself, scrambling out of the warm hole. 'All my friends seem either to be flying off to warmer lands, or finding places to sleep away the winter. I don't want to do either – but yet I *must* find somewhere for a home. And I'd dearly like to have a nice friend I could talk to, too, not one who's going to snore all winter long.'

She met a snake and he invited her to go to a hollow tree he knew and curl up with him and all his friends together. 'We knot ourselves together for warmth,' he said. 'It's a very nice tree we go to, fairy. Do come.'

'Well – no thank you,' said the fairy. 'I like snakes and I think they're very clever the way they glide along without

feet – but I don't want to be knotted up with you all winter. I might want to get out and not be able to, because I'm sure you'd be fast asleep.'

'Oh, we should,' said the snake. 'Well, what about trying the dormouse? He's a nice cosy fellow, and he would keep you warm and not mind a bit if you wriggled in and out of his hole during the winter. He's in the ditch over there.'

The dormouse was very fat. He told the fairy that as he never had anything to eat all the winter, he liked to get as nice and fat as possible before he went to sleep.

'Don't you ever wake up in the winter?' said the fairy. 'I really do want a cosy, furry friend like you to cuddle up

to – but it's so dull having a friend who is asleep all the time and never says a word. And oh dear – I don't know *what* I shall do for food soon. There isn't any honey to be found at all, except in a few odd flowers here and there.'

The dormouse went close to her and whispered, 'I know where there is a store of nuts. Do you like nuts?'

'Oh, yes,' said the fairy. 'Very much.'

'Well, do you see that clump of ivy over there?' asked the dormouse, pointing with his tiny foot. 'I happen to know there are about a dozen nuts there. You could feast on those.'

'Oh, thank you,' said the fairy. She watched the dormouse go down to his little hole in some tree-roots. She liked him very much – but he *would* be dull as a friend, because she knew what a sleepy fellow he was.

She flew to the ivy and found the nuts. She was just wondering how to crack one when she heard scampering feet, and a cross voice: 'Hey! Don't you take my nuts!'

'Oh – are they yours! I'm so sorry,' said the fairy, and put the nut back quickly. She looked at the animal beside her. She liked him very much. He was a red squirrel, with bright eyes and a very bushy tail.

The squirrel looked at the fairy, and he liked her, too. He was suddenly sorry he had been cross, because the fairy looked cold and hungry and lonely. He

took up a nut. 'Would you like me to give you one?' he said. 'I don't like people to steal them, but I never mind giving them away.'

He gnawed through the shell, and got

out the nut. He gave it to the fairy. 'Oh, thank you,' she said, and began to nibble it.

'You seem very hungry,' said the squirrel. 'Where is your home?'

'I haven't one,' said the fairy, and she told him how she had tried to find someone to live with in warmth and friendliness. 'You see - so many creatures go to sleep all the winter - and that's dull, isn't it?'

'Very dull,' agreed the squirrel. 'I think what *I* do is much more sensible. I sleep in my cosy hole when the weather is very bitter, with my tail wrapped round me for a rug - and when a warm spell comes, I wake up, scamper down my tree and find my nuts to have a feast. I have a good play, and then when the frosty night comes again, I pop back to sleep.'

'That does sound a good idea,' said the fairy. 'Sleep the coldest days away - wake up in the sunshine and play, and have a good meal - and go back again when the frost nips your toes. You're the most sensible of all creatures I know, squirrel. How I wish you were my friend!'

'I'd like to be,' said the squirrel. 'You come with me to my hole and sleep with me wrapped up in my tail. And perhaps, in the springtime, when I want to go and find a nice little wife, you'd brush and comb my fur well and make me beautiful.'

'Oh, I *will!*' said the fairy. 'I'd love to

do that. Red Squirrel, let's go to your hole now, I'm cold.'

So up the tree they went and the squirrel curled up in his hole with the fairy beside him. He wrapped his bushy tail round them both and they slept cosily together.

And when a warm spell comes they both wake up and look for the squirrel's nuts. So if you ever see a red squirrel scampering in the winter sunshine, look around and see if you can spy his small companion hiding anywhere.

You *might* see her. You never know!

10

He Belonged to the Family

'You clear away the tea for me, Janet,' said Mother. 'Daddy and I have something important to settle.'

Janet pricked up her ears. 'What is it, Mother? May I listen - or is it secret?'

'Oh no - it's not secret,' said her mother. 'But it's rather exciting. Daddy's going to buy a motor-lorry!'

'A *motor*-lorry!' said Janet. 'Whatever for?'

'To take round the logs, of course,' said Mother. 'Old Brownie's slow, now - and can only pull a small load of logs. Daddy wants to take three times as many out at a time, and so he thinks he'll buy a lorry.'

'Brownie will be pleased,' said Janet. 'He will have a nice rest in the field.'

'Oh, I shall sell him,' said Daddy, raising his head from the advertisements he was looking at.

Janet stared in horror. 'DADDY! Sell Brownie – our dear old horse! Why – I never remember a time without him. Daddy, you *can't* sell Brownie!'

'I've had a very good offer for him already,' said Daddy. 'From Mr. Lucas, down at the farm.'

Janet stared at her father and mother as if she couldn't believe her ears. 'You *can't* sell old Brownie,' she said again, with tears in her eyes. 'Mother – he's one of the family. He really is. I love him. So does Paul.'

'Well, we're fond of him, too,' said her father. 'But we have to be sensible about things, Janet. *I* need a lorry – *Mr. Lucas* will buy Brownie. It all fits nicely.'

'It doesn't, it doesn't,' cried Janet. 'You know Mr. Lucas is horrid. He hits his horses. I've seen him. Oh, Daddy – I can't believe it. Does Paul know?'

Paul was her brother. He was out shutting up the hens, and having a word with Brownie in his old stable.

'No - Paul doesn't know yet,' said Mother. Janet put down the cups she was carrying and rushed to the door. 'I'm going to tell him,' she said. 'He'll beg and beg you not to sell dear old Brownie.'

The door slammed behind her. She ran out into the cold night. 'Paul! Paul! Where are you?'

'Here. With Brownie,' shouted Paul. In half a minute his sister was flying in at the stable door. She caught his arm.

'Paul! Did you know Daddy was buying a motor-lorry – and selling Brownie to Mr. Lucas?'

Paul whistled. 'No! He *can't* do that! Sell our Brownie! Why, he'd be absolutely *miserable!* He loves us.'

'Just at Christmas-time, too,' said Janet, sniffing her tears away. 'Can't you *beg* Daddy not to do such a dreadful thing?'

Paul rubbed Brownie's velvety nose, and the horse nuzzled against him, pushing gently. He loved this boy and girl. The were always good to him, always kind. They had often ridden on him on the way to school when their father had taken his loaded cart of logs to deliver round the town. They were his friends.

Daddy wouldn't alter his mind. 'NO,' he said. 'And please don't be silly over this. I'm not going to turn down a good offer for Brownie. And I do want that motor-lorry. In fact, I've ordered it. It can take three times as great a load as Brownie can pull.'

'Well, Daddy - after all the years of good work Brownie's done for you, I think it's *dreadful* to sell him to that horrid Mr. Lucas,' said Paul. 'You could easily keep him to pull the little cart when you want it. You'll still use it for odd things.'

'Stop talking about it,' said Daddy, getting cross. 'I've made up my mind - and when I do that I don't change it!'

So there was no more to be said! The lorry was to arrive after Christmas, and Brownie was to be walked down to Mr.

Lucas. It quite spoilt the excitement of Christmas week for the two children. They spent all their spare moments with Brownie. They rode to school on him every day, and when he came to the school gate he always stopped.

Then they slipped off his broad back, rubbed his nose, and watched him clip-clop away with the little cart loaded with logs behind him.

'You won't be able to ride on Brownie tomorrow when you go to school,' said their mother. 'Daddy is starting out later, hoping the snow will have melted a little. It's so hard for Brownie to pull the cart over that hard snow up the hill.'

'Oh dear – and it's our last day this term,' said Janet, disappointed. 'We break up tomorrow. After Christmas Brownie will be gone – and we shan't be able to ride him any more! I did so want to ride on him for the last time tomorrow.'

'You can catch the bus with *me*,' said her mother. 'I'm going Christmas shopping tomorrow, and I want to go early. We'll all catch the bus together, and leave Daddy to see himself off.'

So the next day Janet, Paul and their mother set off together to catch the bus. 'Mind how you go,' said Mother. 'It's terribly slippery today!'

So it was! They slithered and slipped down the path to the little front gate, and made their way carefully to the bus-stop. The bus came up and they all caught it. The children got out at the school gate and Mother went on to the shops in the bus.

At home their father finished looking through his order book, wrote a few letters, and then looked out of the window. The sun was out. Perhaps the hard snow up the hill would have melted. He would go out, load his cart, and get Brownie. So out he went, pulling on his thick overcoat.

Just outside the door he slipped and fell heavily. A dreadful pain shot through his right leg. He lay there groaning for a minute or two and then tried to pull himself up. But another pain came and he fell back.

'My leg must be broken,' he thought.

'What shall I do? There's no one in the house. The wife has gone off with the children and won't be back for hours. Nobody will hear me if I call.'

He was so cold and in such pain that he called as loudly as he could, though he knew there was no one to hear him. 'Help! Help!'

No one came. He called again. Then he stopped. What was the good of wasting his strength in shouting when he knew nobody could hear him?

But somebody had heard him! Old Brownie, up in his stable heard his master shouting. He raised his head. He was already puzzled because no one had come to fetch him and fasten him to the cart. He backed out of his stall and turned himself round to face the door. He knew quite well how to open it!

He nuzzled against the latch, trying to lift it with his mouth – and at last he did! He pushed the door. It swung open, and he went out into the snowy paddock.

He could see no one about. He went to

the gap in the hedge and jumped through it. Then he trotted cautiously to the front gate of the little house where his master lived. He put his big brown

head over the gate.

He saw his master lying on the ground! How astonishing! Brownie whinnied a little. The man looked up and saw him.

'Brownie! You got out by yourself – but you can't help me, old fellow!' he said, feebly.

Brownie pushed against the gate but it wouldn't open. He whinnied again, looking at his master. What could he do?

Then he turned and lumbered away up the road. His master groaned again. Even his horse had left him!

But old Brownie had had an idea. There was something wrong with his master. His mistress wasn't there. The children had gone to school. He must fetch one of them.

He climbed the snowy hill, almost falling himself, it was so slippery. He came to the top and went along to the main road. He knew the way quite well. He would go to the school – that place where the children slid off his back each morning, and disappeared.

He came at last to the school gates. They were open. He went in and his great hooves made a muffled clip-clopping sound over the snowy playground. He stopped at the school door. It was shut.

He walked round the building and came to a window. He knew about windows. He had sometimes looked in them before, on his rounds with the cart. So he looked in this one now, but the room was empty.

He went on to the next window – and he looked in that one, his breath steaming the glass so that he couldn't very well see inside.

A class of children were at work in the room. Paul and Janet were there. Paul looked up at the window – and he gave such a shout that everyone in the room jumped violently.

'LOOK! It's our old BROWNIE!' shouted Paul. He leapt up and went to the window. Janet ran too.

'He's by himself. He hasn't got the cart. He hasn't even a bridle on,' said Paul, in wonder. He opened the window and Brownie put his great head in. 'Why have you come, Brownie? Why aren't you with Daddy?'

'Hrrrrrumph!' said Brownie, wisely. Paul looked worried. 'Miss James – please may I go with Brownie? Something must have happened to my father. He should be with him.'

It wasn't long before Paul and Janet were up on Brownie's back, going as quickly as they dared over the slippery snow to their home. And there, on the front path, frozen cold and groaning in pain, they found their poor father!

They dragged him carefully indoors. Janet ran for the doctor. Paul got hot-water bottles and a hot drink for his father. Then the doctor came, and was soon busy setting the broken leg.

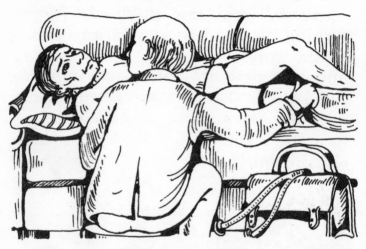

The children watched anxiously, helping in all they could – and somebody else watched too – old Brownie watched through the window, wondering what was happening! The doctor saw the big brown head there and smiled.

'That horse of yours is as concerned about you as much as the children are,' he told his patient. 'Did you hear that he actually walked all the way to their school, and fetched them back here to you to help you? Wonderful old fellow he must be.'

'He *is*,' said the children's father, turning his head to see Brownie's face at the window. 'He heard me calling and somehow got out of his stable to come to me. He put his head over the gate and saw I was in trouble – and off he went. I shall never, never part with old Brownie!'

157

Well! What do you think of *that?* The children cried out in delight.

'*Daddy!* Do you mean that? Aren't you going to get the lorry then?'

'Yes, of course – but I'm going to keep Brownie as well now. He'll run the cart around when your mother wants it for her shopping, and when she wants to take eggs and vegetables to the market. He shall be hers and yours. Can't sell him now, the faithful old friend!'

'Well – *now* Christmas will be lovely!' said Janet happily. 'I felt as if it was all spoilt. But it isn't. Dear old Brownie – shall I give him an extra big feed, Daddy?'

'Yes – all the oats he can eat!' said her father, smiling. 'And a special pat from me. Whatever made me think we could do without Brownie?'

So Christmas was very happy after all. The children had a beautiful Christmas tree, and after tea on Christmas day they lit all the candles on it.

Brownie came to see. They opened the

window for him to put his big brown nose through. He stood there happily and watched the children playing round the tree. There was a present for him, of course!

'Here you are – a carrot from me and an apple from Paul!' said Janet and Brownie munched them hungrily. He belonged to the family. He was happy.

He *still* belongs. I know that because I see Janet and Paul riding him every Saturday!

11

The Little Red Aeroplane

When Uncle Tom, who was an airman, came to see Jimmy's father and mother he brought a present for Jimmy.

'Here you are, Jimmy,' he said, putting a long parcel down on the table, 'I made it for you myself. And it works.'

Jimmy undid the parcel. There was a box inside. He took off the lid and gave a cry of joy. 'Oh, Uncle Tom. It's an aeroplane – a little red aeroplane! Oh, thank you. Did you really make it yourself? What a little beauty!'

'Yes, and it really flies,' said Uncle Tom. 'Let's take it into the garden and you'll see how well it goes.'

So they went out into the garden and Uncle Tom wound up the elastic tightly. When the elastic unwound it would take the aeroplane quite a long way through the air.

Uncle Tom launched the aeroplane - and it flew as high as the tree-tops, circled round and dropped gracefully to earth, almost like a glider.

'It's fine!' said Jimmy. 'I do like it, Uncle. My, won't the other boys be thrilled to see it?'

Jimmy played with his new red aeroplane a lot. He learnt exactly how to launch it into the air, gently but firmly - and how it flew!

'It flies down to the end of the garden, then turns round and comes back again,' he told his mother. 'It's a very *good* little' plane - it seems to know that it mustn't go out of the garden.'

Now one day Alec came to tea. He didn't often come, because Jimmy's mother wasn't very fond of Alec. She said he hadn't any manners and she didn't like the way he always led Jimmy into mischief.

'I wouldn't mind having a naughty boy to tea if *you* led *him*, and not he you,' said Mother. 'But instead of you being strong enough to say "no" to him when he wants you to do something bad you are weak and say "yes". And that's a pity.'

Still, Mother did sometimes have Alex to tea, and he came that afternoon after school. He badly wanted to see Jimmy's new red aeroplane. Mother hadn't let Jimmy take it to school because she was afraid it might get broken there. So Alec hadn't seen it.

But oh, what a pity – after tea it began to rain, Jimmy had just finished having a bad cold, and his mother said she really couldn't let him go out and fly his aeroplane. 'No,' she said, 'you'll get soaked in the rain. Alec must come another day and see it. Perhaps he could come on Saturday morning.'

'Oh, *Mother,* it really isn't raining much,' said Jimmy.

'It's raining quite fast enough for me to say no,' said his mother. 'Now get out your train or something, or you will waste all your time.'

After a while Alec heard the front door shut. He ran to the window of the play-room and looked out. He saw Jimmy's mother going out of the front gate. He turned round, his eyes shining.

'I say, Jimmy. Your mother's gone out. Let's go and fly your aeroplane in the garden. It's hardly raining at all now.'

'No - we couldn't do that,' said

Jimmy. 'Mother would be awfully cross if she knew.'

'She won't know,' said Alec. 'Come on, be a sport. It's not raining very much. Look, can't you see that big bonfire blazing in the garden backing on to yours? Well, that wouldn't be burning like that if it was raining very fast, would it?'

Jimmy looked at the bonfire. It certainly was a fine one. If only Mother hadn't said he mustn't go out he and Alec could have had a good time playing with his aeroplane and looking at the bonfire over the wall.

'Come on!' said Alec impatiently. 'Don't be a baby. Your mother will never know. We'll creep out of the garden door, and your maid won't hear us.'

'All right,' said Jimmy. He did very badly want to fly his aeroplane and hear Alec's cries of delight. 'Better put on our coats, though. Where's my red plane? Oh, here it is, in its box.'

The boys put on their coats. Then, carrying the aeroplane very carefully, Jimmy went downstairs with Alec. They went into the garden. It was certainly raining, but not really very fast - more like a mist than rain.

'Oh, it's hardly raining at all!' said Alec. 'I'm sure your mother wouldn't mind you going out in this.'

Jimmy knew his mother would mind his disobeying her, but he said nothing. He wound up the elastic of his red aeroplane as tightly as he could.

'Now watch!' he said. 'She will fly to the end of the garden, swoop round and come back almost to our feet. She's a wonderful flyer.'

He launched the plane. It did just as he said. Alec watched it with his mouth open in amazement.

'Golly!' he said. 'I've never seen such a wonderful toy aeroplane! Why, it flies almost as well as a real one. Here she comes back again – like a glider about to land.'

The aeroplane came lightly to rest not far from Alec. He ran to it and picked it up. 'My, you are lucky!' he said to Jimmy. 'Fancy having an aeroplane like this. Did you say your uncle made it? Isn't he clever? I do wish *I* had one like this.'

Jimmy was very pleased to hear all this praise from Alec. He took the 'plane from him and began to wind it up again.

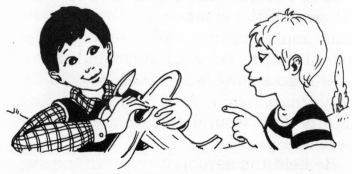

'Let *me* have a turn!' begged Alec. 'Oh, do let me. You might! I bet I could wind it up even more tightly than you can, because I've got bigger, stronger hands.'

So he had. He was a very strong boy indeed. But somehow Jimmy didn't want anyone else to wind up his beautiful aeroplane. 'No', he said. 'I'll do it.'

'Oh, you're mean,' said Alec, turning away in disgust. 'You're selfish. You *might* let me have a turn!'

'All right,' said Jimmy, who always found it very hard to say no to anyone. 'You have a turn, then. But don't you go and break the elastic or anything.'

Alec took the red aeroplane in delight. He wound the elastic up tightly - more and more tightly, till Jimmy was astonished to see him still winding!

'It'll go a long way *this* time and fly very high,' said Alec. 'Just see how tightly I've wound the elastic. Now - here she goes!'

He held the aeroplane high in the air.

He gave it a gentle push and set it free. It rose up - and up - and up! It flew magnificently.

'Look at it!' cried Alec. 'It's going higher than before!'

'It's flying further than our garden! It's turning to come back. Oh, isn't she wonderful?'

The aeroplane had flown high and had gone right over the wall, almost up to the opposite house, whose garden backed on to Jimmy's. Then it turned - but it had gone too far. It hadn't the power to come right back to Jimmy, as it usually did. It fell lower and glided to earth. It disappeared behind the wall in the next garden.

'Come on, quick – we must get it before anyone picks it up!' said Alec and the two boys raced down to the wall. They climbed over it and began to look for the 'plane. But they couldn't find it anywhere.

Someone called to them: 'Hey, what are you doing here?' It was the next-door gardener. He was standing by the bonfire, a long stick in his hand.

'We're looking for my aeroplane,' said Jimmy. 'Have you seen it?'

'Well, something swooped down from the air and hurled itself into the heart of my bonfire,' said the gardener. 'I thought it was a big bird. I've been poking about with my stick to see if I could get it out, but the fire's too hot.'

'Oh, it must have been my aeroplane!' wailed Jimmy and, getting a stick, he poked about furiously – and suddenly he saw a brightly burning red wing!

'Yes, it was my 'plane – and it's nearly all burnt,' said poor Jimmy, almost in tears. 'Look, Alec, there's only a bit of one red wing left. It's gone.'

The two boys climbed back over the wall. Jimmy was trying not to cry. He knew he was too big to cry, but it was such an awful thing to happen. His beautiful aeroplane! To think it had gone into the bonfire like that!

'*Why* did I let you have a turn?' he said, furiously. '*Why* did I come out into the garden to fly it when Mother said I wasn't to? Now see what's happened!

170

You'd better go home before Mother knows about this. She'll be awfully angry.'

But his mother wasn't angry. She was sad and disappointed. 'What a pity to lose such a beautiful aeroplane because you were too weak to say "no" to Alec when he wanted you to disobey me,' she said. 'Be strong another time, Jimmy. Weakness always brings unhappiness. Now your lovely aeroplane is gone for ever.'

So it had. Jimmy was angry and unhappy and very cross with himself. 'Well, *next* time Uncle Tom gives me a nice aeroplane I'll see I don't lose it because of somebody like Alec,' he said to himself. 'I wonder what other children would have done. Would they have given in to Alec too – or not?'

Well – would *you*?

12

Glass on the Road

The boys were planning a bicycle ride to the old pit. 'There will be primroses out there,' said Dick. 'My mother loves those. I'll take her a bunch home.'

'We can throw stones into the pool at the bottom of the pit,' said Lennie. 'That's always good fun – you can see them roll and jump down the steep sides of the pit and then go splash into the water.'

'We'll find some early pussy-willow and take that back too,' said Harry. 'How many of us are going? We'll meet at Breezy Corner.'

There were sixteen boys in the class. Ten of them had bicycles. Harry counted them over, and said: 'Well – that's nine of us. Meet at ten o'clock.'

The tenth boy with a bicycle was little Pat O'Sullivan. John wondered why he had not been asked to join the trip. John was a new boy and he quite liked Pat.

'Why don't you count in Pat?' he said.

'We don't want him,' said Harry. 'You should see his old bike! It's simply awful. I don't like being seen out with Pat – he always looks so funny in clothes that are too big for him – I can't think why his people send him to our school. They are as poor as can be.'

It was true that Pat did look a bit queer always, because he had to wear the out-grown suits belonging to his big brother, and as he was very small, they hung on him as if he were a scarecrow!

173

The bicycle had once belonged to his big brother, too, and was a clanking, rusty thing, whose tyres were always getting punctured.

So Pat was not asked to come. He didn't seem to mind. He was often left out of things like this, but he quite understood that he wasn't as nicely dressed as the others and that his bicycle was dreadful.

The boys met at ten o'clock the next day at Breezy Corner. They had all got sandwiches and something to drink, for they were going to picnic on the sunny side of the pit. It was a perfectly lovely day and the boys were sure there would be early primroses out.

They set off. They hadn't gone more than halfway before they came to some glass on the road. Somebody had dropped a milk bottle and it had broken. There was the glass all over the road!

'Look out!' yelled Harry. 'Broken glass!'

Some of the boys got off and wheeled their bicycles carefully between the bits of glass. Harry was clever and rode in between without touching any at all.

Nobody thought of gathering up the glass and putting it by the side of the lane for the roadman to collect. Nobody thought of the other bicycles which might come by and get a puncture.

They all rode on, talking and laughing. And then John's bicycle began to feel rather bumpy as he rode. He glanced down at his back tyre. Then he gave a shout of dismay.

'I say! I've got a puncture! My tyre is going down. I must have ridden over a bit of glass.'

Everyone got off their bicycles and looked at John's. Sure enough the tyre was flat.

'Blow!' said Harry. 'What a nuisance, just as we were getting on so nicely. Got a puncture-mending outfit?'

'Yes,' said John. 'Wait for me, won't you, because I don't know the way to the pit. I shan't be long. I can easily find the hole. It must be a big one for the tyre to go down so quickly.'

'We can't wait,' said Lennie, impatiently. 'You mend it and come along. You can't miss the way.'

'All right,' said John, rather hurt. 'Don't you wait for me – but Harry, couldn't *you* wait and help me? Just you.'

'Well,' said Harry and stopped. He didn't want to wait. He wanted to go on with the others. 'Well – you can manage all right by yourself, John, and you'll soon catch us up. We want to stop at the little shop at the bottom of the next hill and get some lemonade. We'll wait for you there.'

John said nothing. He had thought that Harry was his friend and would help him. He watched the others get on

their bicycles and ride away, waving. He felt lonely and left behind. Surely *one* of them might have been kind and friendly enough to wait with him.

He got out his puncture-mending outfit from the saddle-bag and opened it. Then he stared in dismay. It was empty! Of course, he had taken everything out to tidy it – and he must have forgotten to put the things back. He remembered now that Dan, next door, had called to him in the middle of his tidying.

'*Now* what am I to do?' thought poor John. 'I can't mend my tyre, I can't catch the others, I shall have to walk all the way home by myself, wheeling my bicycle.'

He heard a clanking noise coming along the road. He turned to see what it

177

was. He saw an old rusty bike coming round the corner and on it was Pat in very old clothes indeed.

'Hallo!' he said, and got off his bicycle. 'Got a puncture? Where are the others?'

'Gone on,' said John. 'And now I find my puncture box is empty, so I can't mend the tyre.'

'I suppose you went over that glass,' said Pat. 'Wasn't it dreadful to leave it all over the road like that? I cleared it all away to the side of the lane.'

John looked at Pat. He felt ashamed to think that *he* hadn't thought of clearing the glass away. Of course, he ought to have done that. It was just like old Pat to do a thing like that.

'I think the others might have waited and helped you,' said Pat. 'Especially Harry, as he's your friend.'

'Where are you going?' said John.

'Oh, out by myself,' said Pat. 'The others never want me with them, you know - I'm too poor for them. I can wait a bit and help you. I always have a

mending outfit with me because my
tyres are so old they are always getting
punctures nearly every time I go out.
Wait a minute, I'll get out my mending
tin.'

Soon the two boys were hard at work
mending John's inner tube. It was
quickly done.

'There you are,' said Pat, pleased.
'Now you hurry and catch up the others.
I'm going to Cuckoo Hill. There are a
lovely lot of wild animals and birds to
watch there. I like it better than the pit –
there's always too many people there.'

'Can I come with you, Pat?' said
John, suddenly. 'I don't think the others
were very friendly to me leaving me
behind like this. I'd like to come with
you. I love watching animals and birds,
too.'

'All right. You come,' said Pat. 'But I
haven't got any sandwiches with me, so
I can't stay long.'

'I've plenty for us both,' said John,

179

feeling happy. It would be nice to have a trip along with Pat. Pat was such a nice friendly person. What did it matter if he was small and wore funny clothes, and had a rusty, clanking bicycle? It didn't matter a bit.

The boys rode off. They went to Cuckoo Hill and had a wonderful time. They watched a blackbird taking little twigs to make a nest. They found the biggest primroses John had ever seen, and some hidden purple violets.

'We'll take some of this pussy-palm, too,' said Pat. 'No, don't hack at it like that, John. You'll spoil it. Let me cut it neatly.'

They watched the rabbits playing in the wood, and saw a wagtail catching early midges over the little stream. Pat knew far more about animals and birds than John did. He was a good person to go out with.

They shared John's sandwiches. John had plenty. Pat said they were the nicest he had ever had.

'Have you got a friend?' said John,

suddenly.

'No,' said Pat, munching away. 'Nobody wants to be friends with *me*. I'm an undergrown shrimp, and my people are poor.'

'Well, will you be *my* friend?' said John. 'I don't like people for the things they have – I like them for the things they *are*, if you know what I mean.'

'Yes, I do know,' said Pat. 'I think like that, too. I like people I can trust, people who are kind and don't mind helping. I'd like to be your friend.'

The other boys were surprised that John didn't join them that day. They rode home in the afternoon and were even more surprised to see John and Pat on the road together, carrying enormous bunches of primroses and a little bunch of violets and some beautiful sprays of early pussy -palm.

'Pat mended my tyre for me, so I went with him,' said John. 'He was awfully decent to me.'

The boys felt rather ashamed. They knew they should have helped John - especially Harry. They came to the place where the glass had been.

'Hallo, someone's been decent enough to kick all that glass to the side,' said Harry.

'Yes,' said John. 'Pat did that when he came along. I don't know why none of *us* did it. It takes somebody really decent to think of a thing like that!'

John and Pat rode off together. 'You know, Pat,' said John, 'it was when you said you had kicked all that glass to the side that I wanted you for my friend. Funny, wasn't it?'

'Yes,' said Pat. 'Well, I'm glad that glass in the road brought me a friend! Good-bye!'

13

A Bit of Luck for a Goblin

There was once a goblin who thought himself very unlucky. He was always moaning and groaning about it.

'Do I ever have any luck?' he would say. 'Do I ever find a spell anywhere? Do I ever have a nice bit of magic given to me? Do I ever have a wish sent to me for my birthday? No, I never do!'

'Well, dear, never mind,' said his wife, who got very tired of hearing the goblin grumble and grouse. 'You've a nice little cottage and me for a wife, and two good suits of clothes, and . . .'

'Stop!' shouted the goblin. 'Do you suppose that's all I want – a tiny cottage – an ugly little wife – only two suits of clothes – and a garden that's always wanting to be dug – and . . .'

'Now, what's all this?' said a booming voice and who should pass by but Mister Tricky. 'Grumbling as usual about your luck, goblin? Why, if you had a bit of luck you wouldn't know what to do with it! You'd lose it with your bad grumbling!'

'I would not,' cried the goblin. 'I'd make the most of it! You should try me and see!'

'Right!' said Mister Tricky and he took a belt from round his waist. 'Look, here's my wishing-belt. You can have it for a while. Take it in turns to wish, you and your wife. And mind you use this bit of luck properly!'

'Well!' said the goblin and his wife gazed in delight at the red belt. The goblin took it. 'This *is* a bit of luck!' he said. 'I'll use it well, Mister Tricky.'

'I'll come and get it back in a little while,' said Tricky and off he went.

The saucepan that was on the stove suddenly boiled over and the goblin's fat little wife gave a squeal. 'Oh! The dinner will be spoilt. Give me the belt, quick, and I'll wish it all right again!'

She snatched the belt and wished for the dinner to be all right. The saucepan stopped boiling over at once. But the goblin was very angry. He grabbed the belt back.

'Fancy wasting a wish on your silly dinner!' he cried. 'How dare you! We can wish for a spendid meal, silly! We don't need to worry about your stew! I wish for a roast duck and green peas!' he yelled.

At once a large dish of roast duck and green peas appeared on the table. 'You're mean,' said his wife. 'You know I don't like roast duck. Greedy pig! Going to eat it all yourself, I suppose.'

'Be polite to me, woman!' roared the goblin. 'Get me a plate and a knife and fork.'

The goblin's wife snatched up the red belt. 'I wish the roast duck was on your head and the peas down your neck!' she shouted, angrily. Well, the wish came true at once, of course, which was most unfortunate.

The duck leapt off the table and balanced itself on the goblin's head, with gravy dripping down his face. The peas emptied themselves cleverly down his neck. He gave a roar and grabbed the wishing-belt.

'You silly donkey!' he cried to his wife. 'I wish you *were* a donkey! Then I could ride you to market and back and save my poor legs.'

Well, his wife turned into a donkey, of course, and there she stood, pawing the floor and braying 'Hee-haw' for all she was worth. The goblin stared in horror. He waved the belt in the air.

'I wish you weren't a donkey,' he said in a tembling voice. But nothing happened, of course, because it was his wife's turn to wish.

He put it on her back. 'Wish yourself back to your own shape,' he begged her. The donkey hee-hawed her wish. But she didn't wish to go back to her own shape. No – she meant to get her revenge on her unkind husband.

'I wish you were a carrot!' she brayed. 'A nice juicy carrot. Then I could eat you!'

And the goblin changed into a carrot, of course. It was very awkward. He lay there on the floor, and the donkey moved up to him. She bared her teeth.

The carrot trembled. The donkey licked him, and had a gently little nibble. The carrot squealed.

The donkey kicked the carrot out of the way, not really meaning to eat him. He fell on the wishing-belt and at once he wished very hard indeed.

'I wish I was myself, I wish I was myself!' And at once he was himself again, with the roast duck on his head and the peas down his neck.

He put the wishing-belt rather humbly over the donkey's back. 'Please wish

187

yourself back, wife,' he said. So she did, and there she stood before him, no longer a grey donkey but his fat little goblin wife.

'We've been silly,' said the goblin, and he took up the wishing-belt. 'I'd better wish away the duck from my head. It

seems as if it's growing there for good!'

So he did – and the duck vanished, though the peas, which he had forgotten, were still down his neck.

'What a waste of a roast duck,' said his wife, who was still angry at being turned into a donkey. She took the belt, and looked at the goblin. 'I wish I had two nice fat cats of my own!' she said. And at once two big black cats came and sat by the fireside.

The goblin flew into a furious temper. "Haven't I told you I hate cats? Haven't I said I'll never have them in my house? I'll wish them away again!'

'Well, if you do I'll wish them back!' said his wife. 'It'll be *my* wish next. Ha, ha!'

The goblin stopped just as he was about to wish the cats away. He had a much better idea than that. He swung the belt and shouted:

'I wish twenty dogs would come into the room! Then they'll chase out your cats!'

Well, no sooner had he wished than the wish came true, of course! Twenty dogs of all shapes and sizes rushed into the room. The cats at once jumped up the chimney! The dogs, sniffing the smell of the roast duck and gravy which hung about the goblin, turned to him and began to sniff at him and paw him.

The goblin's wife ran to pull them away. The dogs, thinking this was a fine game, began to chase the goblin and his wife round and round the kitchen. Oh, what a game they had! Over went the table and the chairs and down went the dishes off the dresser!

'Get the wishing-belt, quick, and wish!' yelled the goblin. But one of the dogs had got it and was rushing out of the door to play with it!

And then, in the middle of all this, in came Mister Tricky, grinning from ear to ear. How he laughed when he saw the chasing dogs and the running goblins.

'Well, well – you seem to be in a bit of a muddle,' he said. 'Where's my wishing-belt? Ah, I see one of the dogs has got it. Here, boy, here! That's right, put it down! Well, well, goblin, what a lot of dogs you seem to have got this morning!'

He buckled his belt round him and went to the door. 'Hi, Mister Tricky!' cried the goblin, trying to push away a big dog. 'Come back! Lend us your belt to wish these dogs away – and there's a couple of cats somewhere, and I've still got peas all down my neck!'

'Keep them!' said Mister Tricky, and walked off, laughing. 'I want my belt now. Ah, what did I say to you, goblin? Didn't I tell you that if you did have a bit of luck, you wouldn't know what to do with it? I was right.'

Poor goblins! They still have the dogs and the two cats, because they simply can't get rid of them. But it really was their own fault, wasn't it, for wasting some really marvellous luck!